BROKEN
UMBRELLAS

KATE SPOHN

Viking

When you walk down the street
you may see her,
because she is always there,
collecting things
that have been thrown away.

You may cross over
to avoid her smell.
Or you may stop and listen
to what she has to say.

She likes to be the talker,
with you the listener.
And this is what she says:
"There is a sale on chocolate at Shop Rite."
"Cut your hair on a new moon
and it will grow back twice as fast."
And, "That 'beautiful woman' is a man."

She offers the use of her cart
to a young woman, a sculptor,
who carries plaster.
"What would I do without you?"
the young woman asks.
"Life would be dull,"
she answers.

Life was never dull for her.
When she was a little girl
she went everywhere
with her father.
She liked walking
to the market with him
to buy food.

Her best friends
were the animals who were sick
and without homes.
She never passed an injured bird
without helping it.

When she was still a little girl,
she left her homeland
and moved to the United States
with her parents.
For some reason they became poor.
But she didn't mind;
she made a game of defeating the bedbugs.
And because she was extremely intelligent
and very curious,
she did well at school.

When she was grown up
she lived where it was warm,
and where herons stood
and where pastel shells lay on the beach.
She taught her native language
at a university there.
Her voice was beautiful,
and she liked wearing stylish clothes
and owning lovely things.

But gradually her life changed.
She dreamed about money.
She hid it under her mattress.
She had conversations with herself.
She saved everything.
She found clothes
that were thrown out on the street
and she hung them on lines in her room.

This was how she became a street picker.
While she looked for more clothes to hang,
she found other things that she liked.
Newspapers, books,
ladders with missing rungs,
bicycle wheels, single shoes, bottle tops,
and her favorite,
broken umbrellas.

She moved to a big city
where there were lots of things thrown out.
She had an apartment that was too crowded
with collected things,
so she dozed in the hall
and slept on the roof in the summer.

She slept only a few hours a night.
Her favorite saying was
"A woman's work is never done."
And she was out and about
before the sun touched the buildings.
She talked to the plants as she watered them.
And she hummed
as she placed more sweaters
in the boxes she put out
for the wild, stray cats.

She found old bread
and shared it with the pigeons.
She was careful that none got onto the street.
She moved along with her cart.
She looked through the trash can,
found a piece of cake left in a box,
and ate it.
Then she folded the cardboard flat
and put it back in the trash can.
She found a headless shower hose
and a book about the painter Edward Hopper,
and put them in her cart.

She looked at the sky,
happy to see that it would rain.
That meant tomorrow would be
a good broken-umbrella day.

She would find them,
colorful and patterned,
lying in the gutter,
on the sidewalk, and in the trash cans.
And she would find her favorites,
the black ones,
the ones that resemble the bats
that are supposed to bring good luck.

She walked along feeling lucky.
Tomorrow would be a good day.

For Regina

VIKING
Published by the Penguin Group
Penguin Books USA Inc., 375 Hudson Street, New York, New York 10014, U.S.A.
Penguin Books Ltd, 27 Wrights Lane, London W8 5TZ, England
Penguin Books Australia Ltd, Ringwood, Victoria, Australia
Penguin Books Canada Ltd, 10 Alcorn Avenue, Toronto, Ontario, Canada M4V 3B2
Penguin Books (N.Z.) Ltd, 182-190 Wairau Road, Auckland 10, New Zealand

Penguin Books Ltd, Registered Offices: Harmondsworth, Middlesex, England

First published in 1994 by Viking, a division of Penguin Books USA Inc.

1 3 5 7 9 10 8 6 4 2

LIBRARY OF CONGRESS CATALOGING-IN-PUBLICATION DATA
Spohn, Kate. Broken Umbrellas / by Kate Spohn. p. cm.
Summary: A woman who spends her time picking up all sorts
of things on the streets didn't always live this way.
ISBN 0-670-85769-6
[1. Homeless persons—Fiction.]
PZ7.S7636Br 1994 [E]—dc20 94-10935 CIP AC

Printed in Singapore
Set in Gill Sans Bold Condensed